LOVE'S FRESH START

LARGE PRINT EDITION

JEANINE LAUREN

LOVE'S FRESH START

Love's Fresh Start was first published in Canada and around the world by Jeanine Lauren. This is a work of fiction. Similarities to real people, places, or events are entirely coincidental.

ISBN: 978-1999070731

Cover design by James, GoOnWrite.com

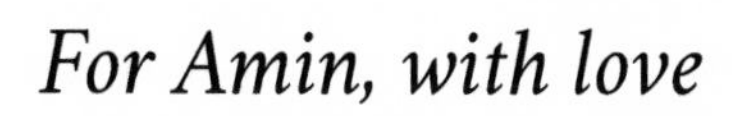
For Amin, with love

ONE

"WHY DID I say I'd do this?" Sylvia Tremblay muttered as she readjusted her scarf to better protect her neck from the chilly spring breeze. She peered up at the steel-grey clouds that covered Sunshine Bay and hoped it wouldn't rain.

Because the doctor insisted that you try walking, the taskmaster in her head answered in a voice that sounded remarkably like her late mother's. A voice that was practical. Bossy. *You must try something. The pills and talk therapy don't seem to be working anymore. Do you want to live like this for the rest of your life?*

As if walking among daffodils and the first buds of spring was going to help her get over this. Mark was gone, and she was alone. She would always be alone.

Stop that. He's gone, and you need to move on. You need to find your old self... the Sylvia you were before this dark cloud settled over you. Before Mark.

Sylvia nodded in agreement with her mother's voice, squared her shoulders against the breeze, and continued to walk.

She had promised the doctor, and now that she was here in the gardens of the city park, she would try to enjoy the morning. It was a normal thing, to take a morning stroll. And it was safer to walk now than in the afternoon. She was less likely to run into people in the morning. She wasn't ready for people yet. Especially men. She hadn't been comfortable around people since Mark's illness and death two years earlier. Since the black…

What was that? Something caught her eye. Small and…

Black.

Sylvia paused in the middle of the path to take in the sight before her, and a small sigh of contentment escaped her lips. How long had it been since she'd smiled? It felt like two long years. And yet here she was, smiling over a little black cat napping in the first rays of warm spring sunshine that had penetrated the clouds above.

Sylvia lowered herself to the bench nearby, happy to find this quiet spot away from people. People made her nervous. But animals, especially this cat…

The cat startled from its sleep and leaped to all four feet. Sylvia jerked in surprise.

"You scared me," Sylvia said. The cat faced her, eyes wary, as it backed toward the underbrush near the path.

"Oh, don't rush off so soon. Here, kitty, kitty." Sylvia rose and stretched out her hand, willing the cat to approach her. The cat turned and ran to the safety of the tangled underbrush, pausing to turn, frozen in place, watching Sylvia.

"You won't get that one to come out," a deep voice said from behind her. Sylvia whirled to see a tall man dressed in overalls, smiling at her from under the brim of a conductor's cap. "That cat's been here for years," he continued. "I see it in the mornings when I come to work. She doesn't like people much. I've tried to be friendly, but she runs away."

"Perhaps she's always been feral." Sylvia's heart pounded. The anxiety that had been her near-constant companion in recent months rose in her chest. She was surprised she could even get the words out.

"I don't think so," the man said. "I was told she belonged to an elderly couple who used to live across the street. They died in a fire a few years back, and she's been here ever since."

"How sad," Sylvia said. She glanced at the cat, feeling a sudden kinship with it. They'd both been yanked from their old world and forced to find their footing in a new one.

"She gets a lot of mice, though. We don't see many at the train station."

"Train station?" Sylvia asked, congratulating herself on her nearly normal-sounding voice as she fought to relax and breathe as if she talked to strange men every day.

"Yes, behind there." The man pointed to a wall of boards painted to appear like a stone fence. "There's a train that runs all summer for the children. I drive it and do some of the maintenance. The season starts in two weeks, so I'm here getting ready for our spring launch."

"The children must enjoy that," Sylvia said, mentally kicking herself for continuing to engage with this man. She wanted to be alone to commune with the cat she was watching. The cat was watching her in return.

"Oh, yes, the children seem to like it. I enjoy it too. Always wanted to drive a train, so I took it up after I retired." He smiled.

"Uh-huh." Sylvia nodded. He didn't look old enough to be retired. He looked about her age.

Was she noticing a man? What would Mark say?

"My name's Jack Robertson." The man extended his hand toward her, interrupting her thoughts.

Sylvia looked at it before slowly shaking. "Sylvia Tremblay." She looked into his hazel eyes that, for an instant, seemed to reveal pain. For a moment Sylvia got lost in that pain. Was Jack feeling as hopeless as she was? Wondering, like her, if that feeling would ever go away?

Maybe he was like her. *Alone*.

Or…

Lonely.

"I haven't seen you around before. Are you new to the area?" Jack asked, breaking into an easy smile in a face lined from a lifetime of laughter. Sylvia found herself returning his smile, hoping hers appeared genuine.

"No, I've lived here for years," Sylvia said. "I don't get to the park often, though." Could he hear her heart pounding? The loud bongo beats in her ears made her momentarily dizzy, and she felt heat rise under the collar of her coat; her face was surely flushed. She felt the heat in her cheeks deepen. Jack glanced at her, then at the cat, and raised his arm to read the time on his watch.

"Well, I should be getting along. Good day to you, Sylvia."

"Yes. H-have a good day." The cold sweat that had begun to climb up her back receded as she watched Jack walk toward the back of the garden and disappear through a door in the fence.

"Well, that was embarrassing." Sylvia seated herself shakily on the bench again and turned her attention back to the cat. "I haven't talked to a man in a while. Except doctors, of course, but they're not the same. Not in their professional capacity anyway." And she would know. She'd encountered an assembly line of medical professionals after the accident and during Mark's extended illness. Sylvia shook her head, pulling herself back to the present. Going down the rabbit hole to the past always led to pain.

Remember the objective, Sylvia. She needed to find her way back to the world, not drift rudderless in a sea of old memories. The cat looked at her, an unblinking statue.

"But enough about me. Tell me,

how do I get you to come out of your shell, little one? You look a bit lean. Haven't you been eating well?" The cat blinked, turned, and walked deeper into the underbrush.

Sylvia sat, staring at the spot where the cat had disappeared, until she became aware that the cold spring air had seeped through her too-thin jacket.

"Well, I guess that's that," Sylvia mumbled. "Time to get moving." She stood and began to walk the path that wound its way through the gardens, glancing into the underbrush intermittently to see if she could find the cat.

When she got to the little bridge that crossed the creek at the centre of the grounds, she paused a moment to watch a mallard duck and his mate drifting in the slow-moving water. Her heart lurched. It was hard to be single when she had so long been part of a pair. She would need to get used to it; there weren't many men interested in a plump sixty-year-old, particularly one with dark clouds invading her every thought. She thought of Jack then quickly dismissed the memory. Just because he was the first man she'd spoken to in months didn't mean he was interested. Maybe he wasn't even suitable. Though he did have a kind face.

At least she wasn't alone in her misery. The online support group she'd found had women from all corners of the Western world bemoaning their new fate. They logged into the chat room or discussion threads, each sharing her story, each one worse than the last. But in some ways, it was a comfort to know other women shared her fate. She was a member of an exclusive club with the ultimate hazing ritual: all you had to do was be the surviving spouse.

Sylvia strolled past an oval track where several men and women walked in a random yet organized pattern, some alone, some in groups, some clockwise and others counter-clockwise, all coexisting despite their different rhythms. People smiled as they passed, and she forced herself to turn toward them and smile in return.

Her doctor would be proud. She'd done what she promised she'd do.

But what now?

Sylvia pulled the bus schedule out of her pocket. If she hurried, she could be home by ten thirty. Where she'd...

Spend time locked in a chat room with other women who were dealing with grief through pills and pity?

No. Today she'd made the effort to come out, and now that she had succeeded, she wouldn't go home right away. Today she would go to the store and buy some necessities: milk, eggs, fresh vegetables, perhaps some cat food.

Resolved, Sylvia walked out of the park toward the small supermarket she normally called to deliver her groceries. It was early on a

Monday morning, and there were few cars parked outside.

"You can do this," Sylvia told herself under her breath. "You've shopped here for years." But she knew it was more than that. This was the first time since Mark's death that she had ventured out to do her own shopping. The bongo beats were back in her ears. *Breathe, Sylvia.* She walked toward the long line of shopping carts, pulled one from its nest, and maneuvered it toward the automatic doors at the front of the store.

The aisles were almost empty, and she soon located the milk and eggs. As she walked past the dairy section, she paused a moment to read the yogurt containers. She had seen ads on television for Greek yoghurt, and before she could talk herself out of it, she picked up a small container. Time for the vegetable aisle.

Sylvia stopped for a few minutes, taking in the colors of the vegetables: red peppers and orange carrots bright against the green beans beside them. Rows of root vegetables and mushrooms—shiitake, white, and portobello. Her stomach gurgled, but she stopped herself from loading her cart. She couldn't be bothered to try new recipes for one. When Mark was alive she had enjoyed cooking for their many visitors, but now…

She took a long, steadying breath and willed the wild bongos to silence. She would stick to the easy food, though she did sneak a bunch of spinach and some lettuce into the basket, along with carrots and red beets to make a fresh salad. Her doctor would be happy to hear that she was attempting to eat healthier. Satisfied, she made her way to the pet food aisle.

There, the bongos returned, and she felt dizzy as she scanned the array of cat food. How would she ever choose? What did a cat like to eat? Pausing a moment to breathe deeply and count to ten, she waited for the anxiety to recede and then examined the options again. Why did she come here? She wasn't ready to be out shopping.

"But what about the cat?" she mumbled. "It's all alone, and skinny from so few meals. You can do this."

There were four different varieties, and she took one of each, placing them quickly into the cart before steering it toward the checkout. Soon she was back outside, holding two newly purchased cloth bags full of groceries.

"You did it," she said, turning toward the street and walking to the nearest bus stop.

JACK WALKED into the shed where the trains were kept. After his winter break, it was good to be back amidst the smell of engine oil and the tools he loved. The train hadn't run since the Christmas season, when he'd driven it through the winter garden brought to life by the lights decorating every branch. He smiled as he thought of the children enjoying the holiday rides. It was one of the joys of his job, listening to them *ooh* and *ahh* over the scene and then cheer when they were herded off at the end to enjoy hot cocoa.

He walked over to the chest and laid out the tools he needed to tune up the engine. Jack loved this part of his job. He used to enjoy tinkering on the weekends before he'd retired from his job as a bank manager two years earlier.

"Hey, Jack." His co-worker, Tyler, greeted him as he stepped through the door. "You're here early."

"Well, I like to get an early start."

"Really? Or is Cassie still smothering you?" Tyler smirked.

"She means well. And it's not as bad as when she first moved back to town." Jack's grown daughter, Cassie, had arrived about two summers earlier, a few weeks after Emma, his now ex-wife, left him.

"Well, it's good to see you and great to be back on the train," Tyler said. "Plus, it beats the landscaping they had me doing the past few months."

"Still planning to take the mechanics course?" Jack asked.

"I've been saving for it since we talked at Christmas. Should have enough by September."

"Good for you, Tyler." Jack slapped the younger man on the back. "A man's got to go after what he wants in life." Or who he wants.

Jack thought back to his encounter with Sylvia. Her hair was a mass of long blonde curls, so unlike Emma's dark red bob, and she wore ordinary clothes, not the high-fashion outfits that Emma had worn the two years before she left him.

Jack tried to focus on what Tyler was saying. Why was he even comparing the two women?

Emma had left. Just like that.

And Sylvia? Pain was there, in her words and expressions. Maybe she was like him, searching for the missing piece that had been missing for far too long.

"I forgot the best part," Tyler said, bringing Jack out of his reverie. "I talked to the boss, and he says there may be a job with the city once I'm done."

"That's great news." Jack was

pleased for his young friend. "Now let's get this engine oiled and ready for the summer."

"All right!" Tyler rubbed his hands together and walked over to where Jack had already laid out the tools. They began to plan the work that needed to be done.

TWO

JACK WALKED HOME, glad to have put in a good day's work. As he passed through the gardens, he saw the little black cat crouched low to the ground, watching a robin. The bird strutted around the lawn, pausing every few steps to peck at the ground. Jack stopped to watch the cat creep toward the bird, her belly close to the ground, ears forward, focused. Jack held his breath as the cat increased her pace and pounced, then shook his head when she landed at the spot where the bird had just been.

"Too bad," he said as she picked herself up and looked at the tree where the robin now perched. The cat turned and walked in the direction of the train station. Hopefully she would find a mouse tonight. She looked skinny after the long winter.

Jack looked around the clearing, half hoping there was someone else who had witnessed the failed attack —a woman with blonde curly hair, someone he could share his thoughts with. The clearing was empty except for the robin that had flitted back to the ground to resume its hunt for worms. Jack brushed away the thought. He might never see Sylvia again, and continuing to think about her was fruitless.

He resumed his walk home, and as he approached the small rancher where he had lived for nearly thirty years, he could already smell the roast beef that Cassie had promised she would make to celebrate his first day back at work.

"Hi, Dad," Cassie said as he entered through the kitchen door. "Dinner's almost ready."

"Thanks, honey." He smiled as he moved past her to the bathroom to wash his hands and change out of his work clothes. He listened as she moved around the kitchen. She was in a good mood. Maybe today they could have a nice meal without all the drama.

Jack joined her at the table as she placed plates heaped with food onto flowered placemats he hadn't seen in ages. Emma had bought them in Hawaii four years earlier, when they had celebrated their thirtieth wedding anniversary. He hated those placemats and made a silent vow to dispose of the things.

"How was your day?"

"We got quite a bit of work done. Tyler's back helping again." Should he ask her the same? What the hell. "How was your job interview?"

"Fine, I think." Cassie didn't look him in the eye. "Not sure I want that job, though."

"What kind of job do you want?" As if he didn't already know. Why couldn't he just shut up? He knew this line of conversation wouldn't end well, and he had just wished for no drama.

"They posted the jobs for kids' summer day camps. If I do that along with the fitness classes I'm teaching, it will give me more experience before..." Cassie took a deep breath, and Jack braced himself. "Dad, I contacted the university and told them I'm coming back in September."

"I see." Jack's heart sank. "So you still have your mind set on this."

"What did you expect?" Cassie looked at him as though he had two heads. "I have to get a career going sometime. I can't just look after you. I'm twenty-two years old."

Jack took a deep breath and

counted silently to ten before speaking again. "You don't have to look after me. I'm not a child."

"No, but you did have a heart attack." Her voice softened. "And I know it's in the back of your mind all the time." Jack couldn't deny that. Though he put up a brave front with Tyler and pretended that Cassie was overprotective, he was afraid of what would happen if she left.

"Isn't there any way you can finish here?"

"Dad, we've been over this a thousand times. I need to move back to Kelowna to finish my courses, or it will take forever. I only have one more year, and if I don't go in September, I'll have to repeat a bunch of classes."

"You say that, but we both know you'll leave and never come back." Jack's voice rose, and he was already ashamed of where this was going.

"Could we just have dinner?" Cassie waved her hand back and forth between them. "Let's just eat."

"You'd probably be happy to move me into a home," Jack muttered.

"Now you're being ridiculous." She sawed off a piece of roast beef, put it into her mouth, and chewed.

But for the sounds of cutlery scraping against china, they ate the rest of their meal in silence. When they were done, Cassie collected the plates and cleared up.

"I'll be back later. I'm going for a run."

Jack nodded as he went to the

living room and settled into his recliner. Taking up the TV remote, he flipped to the news and saw pictures of the familiar face of the TV anchor he had watched for decades, while the young woman now sitting in his chair talked about the anchor's long career.

"He'll be missed as he moves on to another chapter in his life."

"Like hell he'll be missed," Jack grumbled. "He'll be forgotten inside a week."

He looked around the familiar room, the walls feeling too close, too confining.

Nothing in this house was comfortable since Emma had left. What used to be a sanctuary now felt like a prison.

The shelves nearby held photograph albums full of memories he no longer wanted—memories of a life shared with the woman who'd broken his heart.

"I'm going for a walk," he said to the empty room.

Outside in the fresh air, Jack puzzled over what to do about Cassie. He wasn't ready for her to leave, but he felt like a heel trying to get her to stay. He hadn't raised her to be his nursemaid, but he wasn't sure what he would do on his own. The house was too much work for him. Bloody Emma. How could she leave them the way she had? He still felt the punch in the gut as though it were yesterday.

Only six months after the heart

attack that had forced him into early retirement, he had come home, excited to land a new part-time job working on the trains at the park.

Emma was there, dressed to go out, sporting a new coat and a new haircut and colour. She had been going to the gym and wearing clothes that took years off her appearance. He was proud of this new, radiant Emma, and his heart swelled, knowing this beautiful creature was his. Then he saw the two suitcases he'd purchased for a trip to Europe. They had been planning the trip for months, but now the suitcases were sitting beside the door.

"Jack. You're home early." She

looked past him at the closed door, a frown on her face.

"What's going on?" His heart began to pound.

"We've talked about this." She walked past him to look out the window and checked her watch.

"What are you talking about?" But he knew, had known for some time, that things weren't good between them.

"I left you a letter." She waved at the envelope sitting on the mantel. "But since you're here, I'll tell you in person." She took a deep breath and looked him straight in the eye. "I'm leaving you. I realized a few months ago, before you got sick, that I wouldn't be happy retired with you."

Jack felt dizzy. "What are you

saying? We've been planning our retirement for years. You wanted to volunteer at the museum, play golf, maybe take a trip or two. We had our life laid out. Together."

"No, Jack. We've been over this many times. You know I want more than golf and a local volunteer job. I need to spread my wings, see how far I can fly. We've grown apart, and I'm sorry, but I must do this." She was shaking her head at him in… was that *pity*?

"You haven't even noticed, have you?"

"Noticed what?" He was about to say more when the sound of a car horn interrupted him.

"I have to go. Lorenzo is here."

"Lorenzo Baldonado? Your boss?"

"Yes. Don't look so surprised. You must have known that I haven't been invested in this marriage for a long time. And now that Cassie's in college... I can't go on like this, pretending there's something between us. Lorenzo asked me to go with him to Spain for a few months, and I said yes."

"You're having an affair with Lorenzo?" He grabbed the back of a nearby chair and steadied himself. Damned if he would crumble in front of her, but it was tough to stay upright with the floor swaying.

Emma looked at him for a few moments and then spoke slowly and deliberately, as if she was speaking to a child—or even worse, a frail old man. "Don't be difficult. If you think it through, you'll realize this is for the best. We don't have anything in common now that Cassie is grown and gone."

"How long?" How could he not have known? And why wasn't he able to do anything but ask questions?

She moved toward the door now, opening it and putting the suitcases outside on the porch. "I'll be there in a moment," she called and turned to face him. "A couple of years."

"A couple of years?" There he went with another question.

"I have to go. Everything else is in the letter."

"What did you tell Cassie?"

"I phoned and told her that you and I had grown apart—that we both love her, but that we don't love each other any longer."

"How did she take it?" His little girl had finally returned to school after missing a semester after his heart attack. Now she would be thrown into the emotional soup again, and nothing he could do would stop it.

"She sounded surprised, but she'll be fine. It's not like she needs her mother anymore. I told her I'd send her a ticket once we get settled, so she can come and visit. Lorenzo is looking forward to showing her around Spain."

"You know how much she relies on you—on us. She'll be crushed."

"Don't try to make me feel guilty. Cassie isn't a child anymore. She'll get over it." She turned toward the door, pausing for a few moments to look around the room. "I don't know if this will help you make sense of it all or not, but I think of this as a completed marriage, not a failed one."

He stood and stared at her, his mouth open. No more questions. No more words. No more sound.

"Goodbye, Jack. I wish you a good life." And then she was gone. He collapsed onto the sofa, staring at the closed door, and without conscious thought, the sounds trapped in his throat erupted in a howl of anguish that reverberated around the room, continuing until he collapsed from exhaustion.

Over the following months, he discovered that Emma had been planning her escape for a while.

She'd cleared out their savings accounts and sold off some of their assets, leaving him with the house, his pension, Cassie's education account, and a small account that he had been using to secretly save for a gift for Emma: ironically, a three-month vacation to Spain. The note had spelled out her plans in detail, including her assumption that he would sell the house, which amounted to half of their assets.

Jack shook his head to chase away the memories, bringing himself back to the present, where he found his steps had taken him to the park.

As he walked around the gardens, he breathed in the spring air and began to relax. He'd always loved this place and wished he had someone to share it with. Emma had been right about one thing. They didn't have a lot in common anymore.

He couldn't remember the last time Emma had walked in the gardens. She much preferred to walk in the mall, on the city streets, or on the treadmill at the gym. Even when they visited Hawaii, she refused the option of walking in a fern grotto to see the Akaka Falls, missing the scents of fresh hibiscus flowers in favour of sunning herself poolside at the hotel.

As he passed the bench where he'd last seen the cat, he was mildly disappointed not to see Sylvia, who had taken the time to try to coax the wild cat out from the shadows. Something about her stuck with him. Perhaps he'd see her tomorrow. For now, he needed to get home and see that Cassie was all right. She would be home from her run soon.

THREE

THE FOLLOWING MORNING, Sylvia lay in bed. Her right leg ached, and she felt miserable. The sun peeked at her through the slats in the window blinds, urging her to come out and play.

Time to get up, her mother's taskmaster voice said. Her mother had kept moving through life despite losing her first child, her home, five siblings, and two husbands. She had never understood her eldest daughter's infrequent but severe bouts of depression.

"Snap out of it," her mother would say.

Sylvia didn't want to.

That's the depression talking. You need to get up, or that cat will go hungry again.

Sylvia got up. She moved her legs toward the edge of the bed, reluctant to leave the warmth of the covers.

Move it!

"Okay, okay," she muttered, forcing herself to rise, dress, and eat a healthy breakfast. She chose a warmer coat than the one she'd worn the day before and searched her closet until she found a good pair of walking shoes.

She hadn't worn those shoes for three years—not since she was wrenched from her former life by someone who sped through a red light and slammed into her car. She and Mark, who had been driving, were rushed to the emergency room.

Sylvia had awoken in the strict, sterile surroundings of the critical care unit, trying to identify her location, feeling nothing but the fog and extreme thirst that came after a general anesthetic. She felt pain in her right leg. It had been broken in three places, requiring surgery and a full leg cast. Mark was there, waiting for her to wake up. He had walked away with only a few scratches and a dull, persistent pain in his back, something he had felt occasionally before the accident.

She healed quickly and hadn't experienced any ill side effects other than a ghastly scar. *Better a scarred leg than no leg at all,* her no-nonsense mother would have said. *Snap out of it.*

"If only I could," Sylvia said aloud.

The simple song of a thrush pulled Sylvia from her musings, and she focused on the path she had followed the previous day. She breathed in the gentle scent of cherry blossoms and smiled. When she arrived at the bench where she'd noticed the cat, she sank down and leaned forward to scan the bushes, straining to see or hear any sign of movement. Sylvia sat, watching and waiting, and then pulled a can of cat food and a little tin dish from a bag. She opened the can and dumped the contents into the dish, placing the food just under the low-hanging branches of the bushes.

She returned to the bench, her mind wandering. She and Mark had been grateful for their close call.

"I could have lost you," he'd whispered to her as he sat beside the hospital bed, holding her hand.

"I'm not so easy to get rid of," she answered, you aren't going to get out of taking me to France."

He grinned. "Do you want to hear about the catacombs? I found a tour that will take us there for only a few euros."

"As long as you find something cheerful to end the day with," she said. "They buried millions of people down there."

His eyes sparkled with mischief, and he pressed her hand between both of his. "We could go out to Normandy afterward. To see the battlefields."

She shook her head.

"Seriously, I've been looking at the shows as an option. The Moulin Rouge?"

"That sounds lovely," she'd said, before drifting back asleep.

When she returned home from the hospital, they continued to plan. They were to work only thirty-six short months before retiring and embarking on a year-long trip to Europe, Asia, and South America. They'd begun to downsize their house, selling off their bigger belongings, giving away old clothes, books, and gadgets with a forgotten purpose, making room for their new life.

Sylvia shivered as she remembered what came next.

It was August eighteenth when the doctor's office called to say it was urgent that Mark come in for his test results. Mark came home from work after lunch, and she accompanied him to the doctor. "You're better with details," he'd said, but she knew he was concerned. The pain had been getting worse.

Neither of them returned to work. Their days became a whirl of visits to labs for more tests, to doctors for second opinions, and finally to the oncologist, who confirmed the grim prognosis of cancer.

Come on, snap out of it, the taskmaster urged.

"Yes, I know, life is for the living," Sylvia said. She sat a few minutes longer, watching the leaves and waiting for a sign of movement. Disappointed, she walked around the gardens and down the path toward the oval track. There she leaned against a chain-link fence and watched people stroll around the track. Some of them she'd seen the day before. Gathering courage, she walked through the gate, stepped onto the outside ring of the track, and began to walk, smiling at those passing in the other direction. When she'd walked the whole oval, she went back to where she had left the little dish. The food was gone. She sighed happily.

"HELLO AGAIN." Jack stepped onto the path behind Sylvia, startling her. He nodded toward the empty dish. "It looks like you're making progress with the cat."

"It'll take a while yet," she replied, turning briefly to look at him before shifting her attention back to the bush. "But I have patience."

He glanced at the hands clasped together behind her back. No rings. Funny, he hadn't tried to determine a woman's marital status in years, not since before he met Emma. After Emma left, he avoided reaching out to women. The young ones scared the devil out of him with their energy and ideas. The older ones scared him too. They were even more complicated with their past lives and relationships.

He watched Sylvia now as she peered under the leaves. "The cat's lucky you're feeding it."

"I'm lucky she needs my help," Sylvia said. "I haven't had a reason to venture out much in the past few years."

"Have you been ill?" he asked, then mentally kicked himself. Was he prying too much?

"My husband died." She was still looking at the bushes but turned her head to look at him. "I've been finding it hard to begin again. I don't really know where to start."

Her sky-blue eyes welled up with tears.

"I'm sorry for your loss," he said gruffly.

"Thank you," she answered, looking away toward the bush again. "I know people think I should be long past it. In some ways, it seems he's been gone forever. In other ways, well, it seems like yesterday."

"Everyone has to grieve at their own pace." Jack found himself quoting the many people who had told him that when he had lost his parents.

"I suppose they do." She turned again to look at him. Was that gratitude on her flushed face? "I… I had best be going home," she stammered.

He didn't want her to go and searched for a reason to make her linger a little longer.

"Listen, the train will be ready for the spring season in a couple of weeks. Would you like to be the first passenger?"

She nodded tentatively. "I would like that."

"If you meet me here on Monday the week after next around ten in the morning, I'll come and get you."

"Okay," she said. "I'll be here." She turned and began to walk away, then paused and turned back. "Th-th-thank you."

He watched her go, pondering what he had just done. Did a train ride count as a date? Maybe. She looked like she needed a friend, and he was being friendly. He wasn't really interested in a woman who seemed afraid of her own shadow. He stood a little longer, watching her walk away, noticing the way her hips swayed.

"What is it about her?" he asked no one in particular.

"Meow," came a reply, and he turned to see the little cat sitting under the leaves not far from the empty dish. She was licking her paw and washing her face, content after her meal.

"Well, it appears someone agrees with me," Jack said to the cat.

SYLVIA WALKED QUICKLY AWAY from Jack. Had she just accepted a date? No, he was just being friendly. Like those times when people say, "Let's do lunch." He would probably forget all about it by next Monday. But what if he didn't forget?

Well, she would just have to go on a train ride. Where would the harm be in that? So what if she was a grown woman? She told herself to relax and take it one day at a time. If he was there at ten that Monday, he was there. If not, no hard feelings. Meanwhile, she'd continue to feed the cat.

She hoped he would be there. He had kind eyes.

"IT'S DEFINITELY A DATE," Sylvia's sister Alice proclaimed when Sylvia phoned to tell her about her day. "What are you going to wear?"

"I hadn't thought that far ahead. Who knows if he'll even remember?"

"I think you should wear that blue T-shirt. The one we got last fall. The one that makes your eyes pop."

"It's only a train ride."

"And go out and buy a good bra. One that shows off the girls."

"Alice!"

"Don't *Alice* me. You know I'm right. It isn't as though eligible men are falling from the sky. Oh, and make sure you get some condoms. It's not like when we were young. Lots more diseases out there now."

"What would you know? You've been married forever."

"I have friends. I hear stories. Anyway, think about making a bit of an effort. Maybe get your hair done. When was the last time you took the time to pamper yourself?"

"I'll think about it. And... Alice? Thanks."

"Anytime, Syl. I'll talk to you in a few days. I'm glad to hear you're getting out again. I've been worried about you."

When she hung up, Sylvia grimaced. Trust her sister to make a big deal about a little thing. She picked up the phone again and dialed Elaine. She hadn't heard from her stepdaughter in weeks. In fact, Elaine rarely called anymore. She had called more often when she first began to get gigs and sing professionally, to share her successes and her failures. She had a steady job now, singing in a band that travelled a circuit, performing in venues in Vancouver and sometimes Toronto or Montreal.

Elaine was living and loving her life, and Sylvia was proud of her, though she did miss hearing from her. She was playing in Toronto these days, and with the time difference, it was more difficult to connect.

Maybe, she thought, Elaine didn't really want to hear from Sylvia anymore. Elaine had once been very close to her, before Mark died. Before her mother came back into her life. *Oh, go away,* the taskmaster answered. And she was right. There was no need to jump to conclusions. Elaine was probably just busy...

The call went to voicemail, and Sylvia left a brief message. "Just thinking about you and thought I would see how you're doing."

Forcing thoughts of Elaine out of her mind, she wandered to her office to log in to the depression chat room, but she soon found herself surfing the Internet, reading customer reviews of nearby hair salons. An hour later she made an appointment for a cut and color the following week. Alice was right. Although she hadn't said it directly, Sylvia knew she had let herself go over the past few years. It was time to put some effort into her appearance, to look after herself again.

Sylvia travelled to the park over

the next few days, bringing cat food and emptying it onto the little tin dish. Every day she moved the dish closer and closer to the bench, and every day the dish was empty when she returned from walking the oval track. Her stamina was increasing, and she was now walking five times around the oval and looking forward to her new routine.

On Sunday, she noticed a folded piece of paper under the tin dish. It was probably from Jack. Cancelling their train ride, she assumed. She had been looking forward to it. Glancing around to see if anyone was watching, she opened the paper and read the words that had been written in perfect cursive.

Hello, I notice that you feed the cat every day. I just lost my cat after many years and have cat food that I'd like to donate. Could I arrange to meet you and give you the food?

Sylvia glanced to her left and right but saw no one watching. Carefully she refolded the paper and pushed it into her pocket.

She opened a can of cat food and emptied it onto the dish, placing the dish slightly behind the bench. She sat again, considering how to respond to this unexpected correspondence. She pulled a pen and small notepad out of her pocket—she had been carrying them with her since Mark first became ill, to write down instructions, medical terminology, and to-do lists.

She began to write.

I am sorry you lost your cat. I know how difficult it is to lose those you care for. I think that this cat would welcome the food you have. Would you like to share the feeding?

She paused a moment and, taking a deep breath, added her cell phone number to the bottom of the note. She folded it quickly, went to the dish, shoved it underneath, and walked away. She glanced back only long enough to notice that the cat had crept out of its hiding place and was devouring the contents of the plate.

Sylvia climbed onto the bus shortly afterward, reminding herself to breathe so the anxiety didn't creep into her brain and start her heart palpitations again. What had she been thinking, leaving her phone number on a note in the middle of the park? What if the writer was an axe murderer? Or... Or what?

The psychologist she had seen after Mark died had told her about ANTs: Automatic Negative Thoughts. She needed to kill them by questioning their validity. Perhaps she had not been particularly smart to leave contact information for a stranger, but really, what was the risk? She had given her cell phone number. Her land line, not her cell, was the one connected to her address. She could change the number if anything happened. Besides, how many axe murderers had perfect penmanship?

She took a few moments to breathe deeply, thinking through the situation. Most likely the person was just trying to help and get rid of old cat food. She might as well take the note's author at their word. She began to relax, and the anxiety that had been spreading up to her chest subsided. *Think positive thoughts. Don't let the negative thoughts in. It's just the depression talking again.* As she listened to the warring voices in her head, she was glad no one could hear them, or they would know she was going crazy.

Sylvia looked out the window and watched the buildings go by. The distance to her neighborhood was relatively short, only two or three miles. Perhaps she should try walking to the park tomorrow. Or riding a bike. Could she ride a bike? She had sold her bike after she married Mark. He preferred to jog or swim instead. Ten years was a long time, but taking it up again was supposed to be, well, like riding a bike.

A few hours later her cell phone rang, and she reached for it, expecting it to be Alice or Elaine. Instead a reedy voice at the end of the phone said, "I'm phoning about the cat."

"Oh, you're the person who left the note."

"My name is Isabella. I'd be happy to share the feeding of the cat, but I only go out early these days."

Sylvia talked to Isabella long enough to set a time to meet the following day. "I'll show you the routine, so we can keep building the cat's trust," she said. "And I would love your ideas. I've never tamed a wild cat before."

She took care getting ready the next morning. She defrizzed her curls and put on some makeup, rubbing it off twice before getting it right. It had been so long since she had put on blush or mascara, she was all thumbs.

She considered her reflection. She looked good, and she hoped the trip to the salon would further improve her confidence. Her anxiety had been at bay all morning. She was going to meet a woman about the cat, and then she was going to the salon. Normal things for a normal day. Nothing to be anxious or worried about.

A tiny elderly woman was sitting on the bench when Sylvia arrived.

"Isabella?"

The woman turned toward her,

and Sylvia realized she had been mistaken. This woman was about Sylvia's age. She beamed and rose to shake Sylvia's hand.

"I'm pleased you responded to my note. I felt rather silly, but my daughter told me I had nothing to lose, that I had to reach out or stay stuck indoors forever. My husband died recently." Her face reddened. "But you don't need to know that. Why don't you tell me about the cat instead? Does it have a name?"

"Angel. I named the cat Angel. And I know how hard it is to start over when you lose someone you care about. I lost my husband two years ago, and ever since, life has felt empty. But then I happened upon Angel."

Isabella smiled. "You do understand. Thank you for saying so." She reached into her bag and pulled out a can of cat food.

"Oh, she seems to really like that brand. How wonderful," Sylvia said when she saw the tin. She showed Isabella the routine that had begun to build the cat's trust. "I'm hoping that by summer she'll trust me enough to let me take her to the vet and make sure she has her shots and is spayed. I'd like to be able to get her indoors before winter comes."

"Admirable goals," Isabella said. "I'm happy to help." And with that she picked up the small dish and loaded it up with cat food, placing it behind the bench, a little closer than where it had been the day before. "Do you come every day to the park just to feed the cat?"

"When I first started to come a few weeks ago, it was to get some fresh air. And, yes, I suppose I did come to feed Angel. But now I stop over at the track past the trees and walk before I go home again."

"I didn't know there was a track." Isabella was grinning. "I used to be a runner. Before. Well, before my husband got killed. Would you mind showing me where it is?"

Sylvia led the way across the park, and the two women walked together for several laps.

"I've always wanted to run the Boston Marathon," Isabella said. "I haven't run for years."

"It's been a long time since I've even considered what I want to do," Sylvia said. "I always wanted to travel more. My dream was to go to

Italy on a culinary tour, and once, when I was much younger, I thought it might be fun to ride a bike around one of the Gulf Islands."

"What's stopping you? There must be groups of people who take bike trips together."

"I have to learn to ride a bike again first." Sylvia laughed. "It's been forever since I rode even a stationary bike. Besides, I have to befriend Angel."

"Thank you for letting me share her," Isabella said. "It's been a long time since I had anyone, or anything, depend on me. It's good to have a reason to get up in the morning."

They said their goodbyes, and Sylvia felt lighter than she had in months. *I may have just made a friend.*

She fought off the usual negative thoughts and looked at her watch. She'd have to run to catch the bus. She didn't want to be late for her appointment at the salon.

FOUR

WHEN SYLVIA ROSE from the salon chair a few hours later, she ran her fingers through the curls of her new bob. The grey was gone, and her head felt light, as though a weight was lifted with her long tresses gone. She stared at the mirror for a long moment, having trouble believing it was her own reflection staring back.

"You've changed my appearance completely," she said to the young woman who had cut her hair. "I look like the old me." *The me before Mark got sick. The me before...*

In the back of her mind, she wondered if it really mattered what she looked like, since no one was likely to notice anyway. But she closed her eyes and shook off the memories.

Don't listen to the depression, her strong voice said. *Don't let it win today.*

She ran her hand through her hair again. She looked great, and she'd begun to make a new friend. Today was a good day. She pasted a smile on her face and walked toward home. She was going to stop off at the grocery store to get some fresh vegetables, pull out her favorite cookbook, and make a nice dinner. Even if she was alone, she deserved a good meal.

JACK GRUMBLED as he walked home, his stomach growling. Cassie had announced three evenings before that she would be working with the kids' day camps that summer. She was going to a planning retreat for the week.

"I'll have to be away for five nights, Dad. If you need me, you can call the office. They'll get me the message."

He didn't have a lot of say in the matter and told her he'd be fine. But he'd woken up late and had forgotten to make his lunch the night before. Then he'd left his wallet on the bedside table, and Tyler had called in sick. He'd planned to borrow a few bucks from his young friend. His stomach growled, reminding him that he had miscalculated the day entirely.

Arriving home, he went straight to the fridge to root around for something to eat. He didn't mind cooking, but he rarely had the chance. Emma had hated his cooking, and since Cassie had returned, she'd taken over that task. *Damn.* The fridge was nearly empty. Emma would never have left it this way, but Emma was gone, and Cassie was away too.

"Argh!" He went into his bedroom, changed out of his overalls, grabbed his wallet, and headed out. He'd have to go grocery shopping.

Jack steered the cart toward the edge of the supermarket, remembering what the nutritionist had told him. He was to stick to the edges of the store, where the fresh food and dairy were found, and avoid the middle aisles with the processed food. He placed a selection of colorful vegetables into the cart and walked toward the meat section.

As he rounded the corner, his cart grazed another.

"Pardon me," he said, and looked up to see bright blue eyes peering back at him. His heart skipped. "I wasn't watching where I was going."

Sylvia stopped and stared at him

before she seemed to find her voice. "Jack! How are you?"

"Hungry, if you want to know the truth." He answered without thinking. "My daughter—I mean *I*—forgot to go shopping this week."

She peered into his cart and smiled up at him. "It looks like you have a good selection. What are you making?"

"I haven't the foggiest idea. I'm not much of a cook."

"Well, there are all kinds of possibilities in that basket," she said. "You just need to search for recipes on the Internet that go with the ingredients you have."

"I can't say I've ever done that. I'll have to get someone to show me one day."

"I can show you. I-I-I mean… if

you have a few minutes, perhaps we can go to a coffee shop and I can show you on my phone. Most coffee shops have wi-fi."

"How about we go one better? How about I take you to dinner? There's a little Greek restaurant near here that I heard is very good."

"Oh... I'm not really dressed to go to a restaurant."

She looked down at her jeans and T-shirt, and his eyes followed hers. She looked just fine to him, and he said so.

"I was going to go home and cook dinner."

"Of course, I didn't think. You must have someone at home to cook for."

"No, no. It's not that. I mean, no,

I don't have anyone waiting. I was just going to cook for myself."

"Would you join me for dinner?" he asked. "Then you can show me how to find the recipes, and I'll be prepared for tomorrow night."

Emotions flitted across her face. He loved watching her make up her mind.

"Well… Yes, I would love to have dinner with you." She looked relieved to have made the decision. "But first, I need to pay for my groceries."

"Great!" Jack said, a little more loudly than he wanted to. "I'll meet you out in front of the store in, say, fifteen minutes?"

He pushed the cart over to the meat section, selected some lean meat, and took a detour to pick up a small bouquet of tulips. Sylvia seemed like the kind of woman who would appreciate flowers.

When he pushed his cart out front, he found her on the corner, looking up at a tree.

"He's a saucy thing," she said, pointing to a grey squirrel high in the branches above her head. "He's been teasing the birds." She was smiling widely, and Jack found himself chuckling and sharing her delight. Emma would never have noticed the squirrel. She moved through life at breakneck speed.

He paused a moment longer, watching Sylvia. She was beautiful. How had he not noticed that the first time they'd met?

"You've cut your hair."

She lifted her hand toward her head. "Yes, I decided I needed a change."

"I like it."

"Thanks." She blushed, and he was pleased. It had been a long time since a woman had blushed in his presence.

"Shall we go to the restaurant?"

He led her to his car and opened the passenger door for her before loading their groceries into the cooler bags Cassie insisted they keep in the trunk. As he slid into the driver's seat, he reached over to hand her the tulips he'd purchased.

"I thought you might like them," he said, feeling a little shy.

Sylvia brought the bouquet close to breathe in the scent. "Tulips are one of my favorite flowers," she told him. “They come in so many colors and brighten up the world after the winter is done.”

“Have you ever been to the tulip festival in Washington state?”

“No, but once, a long time ago, I went to the one in Agassiz. There were acres of flowers. It was breathtaking. And you?”

“Unfortunately, I haven’t travelled as much as I would like, except for the occasional trip for work.”

“Where would you most like to go?” she asked

“France, I think. I always wanted to see Paris.”

“Mark and I had planned to go there this year but, well…”

“You could still go,” he said. Mind you, he didn’t think he’d ever go to Spain. Not now that Emma had ruined it.

"I suppose I could. But where I really want to go is Italy. With all the movies about Tuscany, and the shots of the vineyards, I think it must be a wonderful place to visit. All that amazing food. I'd love to take a culinary tour."

"For tonight, we'll have to settle for Greek fare." He pulled the car into the restaurant lot.

"Perfect," she said. "I'm starved."

And he realized he had been enjoying her company so much he had forgotten his hunger.

They lingered over dinner, sharing stories. He told her about his job at the bank, his new work with the trains, how he mentored Tyler. She told him about her life as a teacher before she had left work for good. They talked about their families, their childhoods. She told him about Elaine and Alice, and he told her about his daughter.

"Cassie sounds like a wonderful girl."

"She's my great joy."

"And what would she like to do for a living?"

"She wants to be a teacher," he answered. "In fact, she only has a year of classes left."

"You must be proud."

And he was in that moment. He was proud of his daughter and truly wanted her to get her teaching degree. In Sylvia's presence, he felt this was a real possibility. She made him feel less lonely. Less needy. He felt like his old self for the first time in a very long while.

The waiter began to hover as they drew out the evening with conversation. "Could I get you anything else?" he finally said. "We're about to close."

"Oh." Sylvia looked out the window at the darkened garden in front of the restaurant. "I don't think the night has passed this quickly in a long time." She reached for her purse.

"Please," Jack said, placing his hand on her arm. "Let me get dinner."

She looked up into his eyes and smiled. "All right, as long as you allow me to cook for you one day soon. I'm a really good cook."

He drove her to her house and

paused a moment before getting out of the car to open her door. She was already standing on the sidewalk, holding the tulips and ready to get her groceries.

"Thanks again for dinner," she said. "I had a lovely time."

"Thank you for joining me—and for being such charming company."

She blushed again, and he found himself pleased. Pleased that he was the reason she was flustered. He grabbed her second bag of groceries and offered to carry them in.

"It's okay—I've got them," she said. "I'll see you next Monday?"

"Ten o'clock." He watched as she walked up to her little house, reached into her pocket for her key, and let herself in.

He couldn't wait until next week.

SYLVIA HEARD the beeping of the message machine as soon as she got inside. Alice had called more than once while she was out, and the third call had only been thirty minutes earlier. Her sister sounded decidedly worried, so Sylvia dialed her number.

"Hi, Alice. Sorry to call this late."

"Thank God! I was worried. Where have you been?"

"Well, I was out on a date with Jack."

"Jack? The train engineer Jack? I thought you were going on the train ride next week."

"I ran into him at the grocery store. It was an impromptu thing. Anyway, he took me out for dinner."

"Eeee!" Alice squealed, reminding Sylvia of their childhood. "Spill. Tell me everything."

There was a knock at the door. Sylvia frowned and sidled over to the window to peek through the blinds. Jack stood on the porch, her purse in his hand.

"Listen, it's getting late. I'll call you tomorrow, okay? I just wanted to let you know I got home safely."

"All right, but I want details!"

Sylvia hung up and went to the front door.

"Hi," he said. "You forgot your purse, and I remembered... Well, I forgot to get your phone number."

"Hi," she said in return, grinning

at him as though she were a teenager with a crush. *Don't be such a twit, Sylvia. He's just being nice.*

She told her depressed brain to shut up and go away. She wasn't about to let it ruin the evening for her.

"Thanks for bringing it back," she said. "I don't know what I would have done when I realized it was missing."

He looked into her eyes, silently waiting. Her heart pounded.

"Would you like to come in for a coffee or tea?" she said, breaking the silence.

He stepped across the threshold before she could change her mind, dropped her purse on a chair near the door, and then took her face in his hands. He leaned in and whispered, “And I forgot to kiss you goodnight. May I?” She nodded slightly before his lips descended on hers, questioning at first and then gaining force as her hands crept up his chest and around his neck.

His hands left her face and slipped down her back, pulling her closer as he deepened his kiss. A long moment later, they broke apart. “That was even better than I imagined,” he said, and she felt the heat of a blush rise to her neck and cheeks. “Now, before I leave, how about that phone number? I’d really like to be able to call you later.”

She laughed at the earnest look on his face, and a little thrill went up her spine. She had forgotten what it was like to be desired by a man.

It's not you he desires. His wife left him. He's probably just lonely. Her depressed thoughts intruded on her glow.

"Let me get a pen and paper," she said leading him toward the kitchen. As she wrote her name and number on a pad of paper near the telephone, she watched him survey the room.

"You weren't kidding about liking to cook, were you?"

"Nope. I love trying new recipes. When I left my job, I think my co-workers missed my potluck dishes more than they missed me. Here you go. My number."

He took the paper from her hand and then pulled her close for a second kiss. "I'll skip the coffee, if that's okay. I have to go to work in the morning, and caffeine keeps me awake."

"A rain check, then." She made a mental note to get some decaf. She closed the door behind him, hugged herself, then danced into the kitchen to put away her groceries—and put her flowers into water.

FIVE

THE FOLLOWING DAY, Sylvia was on the bus on her way home from the park when she noticed a Canadian Tire store, and on impulse she got off at the next stop. She'd look and see if they had a sale on bikes. She had some insurance money, and she'd never replaced their car, because she hadn't the courage to get behind the wheel again after the accident.

With a bounce in her step, Sylvia walked into the store and scanned the signs above the aisles. Not seeing the bikes, she moved to the seasonal aisle, and there they were in bright red, pale blue, and metallic green. Which one? Any at all? How much should a bike cost? Should she comparison shop? Maybe she couldn't ride one anymore. Why did she get off the bus? Was it going to rain before she got home?

She quickly saw that the choices were fewer than she anticipated. Some were for children, others for men. She looked at the four models that were nearer her size and decided to try the powder blue one at the end. She pulled the bike forward, straddled it, and kicked up the kickstand. She used her feet to push the bike along the aisle then stopped to look at the price tag. Fifty percent off. She climbed off the bike, walked down the aisle, and found a helmet that matched. She hadn't indulged in color-coordinated accessories for years. Then she found a basket for the bike. She liked the idea of having a bike like Angela Lansbury's in the old TV show *Murder, She Wrote*—one that she could ride through the lanes, carrying her shopping in the little basket in front.

"Can I help you?" a man asked from behind her. Startled, Sylvia jumped and, taking a calming breath, turned to see a young man in a store uniform smiling at her expectantly.

"Yes," she said. "Could you please

tell me how this basket attaches to that bike?"

"May I?" he said, taking the basket from her. He turned it over in his hands and fastened it easily to the front of the bike.

"Pretty easy," he said, showing her the mechanism she would need to attach and detach the basket in moments.

"So it is," she said, smiling. "I'll take it."

He nodded and began to remove the basket.

"Oh, no," she said. "I'll take it all." She placed the helmet in the basket and pushed the bike toward the checkout area.

Looking in the plate-glass window outside the store, she took the time to put on the helmet and check it for fit. Her newfound courage almost escaped her as she stood looking at the woman in the mirror of glass. Discarding the helmet's packaging inside the store was a rash decision she was beginning to regret as she fumbled with the straps. What was she thinking? She would never be able to ride a bike as well as she had in her thirties.

No more ANTs, she reminded herself, and then, looking pointedly at her reflection, which seemed to agree with her, she gripped the handlebars, straddled the bike, and kicked up the stand. She would try here in the quiet parking lot, away from unexpected cars and prying eyes. She pushed off tentatively with her left foot. Wobbly at first, she began to pedal, smiling as the breeze brushed against her face and navigating around the lot without incident. She gripped the brakes on the handles slowly, bringing the bike to a stop in front of the store window.

Could she ride home? The side streets weren't very busy between the store and her house. What else was she going to do? She didn't want to figure out how to load the bike onto the front of the bus. Steeling herself, she gathered her courage and pedaled toward home.

Once there, she turned on her computer to check her email—the only messages were from the grief chat room. She replied to a few. One woman she often corresponded with had been anxious about Sylvia venturing outside.

"What if something happens to you?"

Sylvia smiled as she answered. "Something did happen. I went on a date, and I bought a bike." Then she logged off the computer, made a cup of tea, and settled down to read a book.

SIX

SYLVIA DRESSED CAREFULLY to go to the park the next day, wondering —hoping—that she might run into Jack. She'd bike there. She'd thought about biking quite a bit since her conversation with Isabella and hoped that having a goal might motivate her more. If, at sixty-plus, Isabella could train for the Boston Marathon, then there was no reason she couldn't train for an event too. She surfed the Internet and decided that her first bike trip would be to one of the Gulf Islands later that fall. She'd plan which one later, but meanwhile, she would bike an hour or so a day to build up her stamina.

She rode around one of the bike trails in the park for a half hour before riding up behind a man with a familiar gait wearing overalls and a conductor's cap. Now that he was there in front of her she slowed a bit, waiting for the anxiety rising in her chest to subside.

"He's just a man," she whispered to herself. A nice man. And a great kisser. *He isn't interested in you. He's just lonely.*

Maybe at first he'd just taken the time to talk to a stranger about the fate of a little cat. But that kiss? It had desire behind it.

She pedaled a bit faster, planning to casually run into him. He was getting closer to the parking lot now and patting his pants pocket, probably looking for his keys. He would be gone soon, and she'd miss her chance.

As she put on speed—just enough to appear casual and not like she was chasing the man—he stopped abruptly and pivoted on his heel to face her.

"Jack!" she said, braking hard. "Ahhh!" She managed to dodge him and a young woman pushing a baby carriage before she lost control and crashed onto the paved bike path. She lay there a moment with the air knocked out of her.

"Sylvia?" he said as he ran up to her. "Are you okay?"

She tried to disentangle herself from the bicycle and winced at the pain shooting through her right leg. "I'm not sure. My leg. I think it's broken."

The woman with the baby carriage had stopped to see the commotion and offered to phone the ambulance. Sylvia lay back, feeling grateful that someone was there to help and at the same time stupid for riding too fast.

"Can you move?" Jack asked as he knelt beside her.

"No. I'm sorry, you must have other things to do."

"Don't worry about me," he said. "It's not every day a beautiful woman literally falls at my feet."

She looked up into his face and smiled through her pain. "I bet you say that to all the girls who crash their bikes in the park." Was she flirting? God, she was lying completely helpless on the ground, and she was flirting.

He chuckled. "So far it's only happened the one time." He sat beside her, talking and gently moving his hands over her arms and legs to see where the pain was coming from. When he got to her right leg, she squealed. "Yep, it looks like this leg is the culprit. I'm going to leave this to the professionals. Do you hear that siren? Hang in there. The ambulance should be here any minute now." As if on cue, the ambulance drove into the parking lot, and two uniformed attendants jumped out and rushed over to her.

"Thanks for waiting with me," she said to Jack.

"Not a problem," he answered. "Listen, if you need anything at all, give me a call." He rooted around in his pocket and pulled out a small pad of paper and a pen. "And if it's okay with you, I'd like to call and check up on you."

She nodded weakly. "I'd like that," she said, and he tucked the paper with his number into her jacket pocket.

"Meanwhile, call if you need anything. I mean *anything*." He waited until the paramedics separated her from her bike and transferred her to the stretcher. "I'll keep this at the station until you're able to ride again." He patted the bike.

She willed the paramedics to move faster and get her into the ambulance quickly. She didn't want to break down in front of Jack.

Finally, they opened the back door of the ambulance, pushed her stretcher inside, and closed the door on the several onlookers who had gathered to watch. The last face she saw was Jack's, worry etched on his brow as he gave her a little wave.

For the next twelve hours, Sylvia experienced a severe case of déjà vu as she entered the emergency room, was prepped for surgery, and woke up in recovery before being shipped to a bed on the acute care ward. The difference was that this time, she was alone.

Mark wasn't there to greet her when she woke up.

"Good morning, Mrs. Tremblay," a nurse chirped. "How are we feeling today?"

Sylvia looked up at the woman who was no more than a girl and silently took stock of exactly how she did feel. "My leg hurts like the devil, but otherwise I seem to be in one piece."

"The doctor will be here in the next hour to review your chart with you. You can be discharged after breakfast, and the social worker will meet with you to make sure you have home care. Take this medication for the pain, and someone will bring a tray in to you in a few minutes."

"May I have my cell phone?"

Sylvia asked, and the nurse obliged by retrieving a plastic bag attached to the end of the bed. She pulled the phone out of the bag and turned it on. Nothing happened. The battery was dead. How would she phone Isabella now? The poor cat would think they'd abandoned it again.

The nurse patted her on the hand and told her not to worry. There were spare cords at the nurse's station, and she would send one down with breakfast. "What we need to do now is to get you up and dressed. Get you to the bathroom. Do you think you can void?"

Sylvia told her she would try and marveled, not for the first time, at how fixated those in the medical profession seemed to be on bowel movements. She struggled to shift her weight and swing her legs to the edge of the bed, took the proffered crutches from the nurse, and wielded them efficiently to the bathroom unassisted. "Unfortunately, I have a lot of experience with these," she told the nurse, who hovered nearby. "I'll be okay on my own." The nurse waited until Sylvia got into the bathroom and left, satisfied with Sylvia's assessment of her ability.

"I'll be okay on my own," Sylvia repeated to her reflection in the bathroom mirror as she pondered what she needed to order for food and how she would get work done around the house while on crutches. It would be challenging, especially for the first couple of weeks, but she was sure she could manage. She'd managed worse.

She settled back into bed just as the kitchen staff brought her breakfast and the promised cell phone charger. She plugged in the phone and waited for it to spring back to life. There were five messages: two from Alice and three from another number she didn't recognize. Before Alice, she dialed Isabella's number and told her what had happened.

"I'll be happy to feed Angel every day until you're better," Isabella assured her, and she admitted that yes, she had been training and was able to run ten kilometers now.

"That's wonderful!" Sylvia said, sitting up too fast and wincing as her leg protested. "I'll call again in a few days to let you know when I'll be back at the park."

Then, with a deep sigh, she dialed Alice's number.

"It's about time you called. Have you been out on another date?" Alice sounded annoyed, and Sylvia began to feel defensive. Why did Alice treat her like a child?

"Actually, I had an accident." She heard Alice gasp. "I'm okay. I fell off my bike and broke my leg again."

"What were you doing, riding a bike at your age?"

"What's that supposed to mean? I'm not ancient and decrepit."

"Oh, Sylvia, I know that. I've just been worried that you were out with that man again, and that he wasn't as nice as you thought he was."

"I appreciate that you worry about me, but I'm a grown woman."

"I do worry. You're my only sister."

"I'll be fine."

"How bad is the break?"

"It's pretty bad, but only in one place this time. They operated on me and put in a couple of plates. I'm in the hospital, waiting for the surgeon."

"You can come here while you recover. I'll come and get you."

"Don't bother. It would take you hours to get here, and it's not necessary. Wait until I talk to the doctor, okay?" Sylvia was surprised at the anger she felt. Alice was being overbearing, and for the first time in a long time, Sylvia realized she didn't want to answer her sister's questions or give in to her way of thinking. She certainly didn't want to go to Alice's house and be waited on like an invalid.

"If you need me, call me. I have some vacation that I can take."

"I will," Sylvia promised, ending the call with a groan. She knew why she was angry. Mark wasn't there, and she didn't want to be dependent on her sister. She closed her eyes at the memory of nursing him for several months before giving in to his request and surrendering him to the hospital for twenty-four-hour care.

One morning she'd found his ex-wife in the hospital room, talking to him as only someone with a shared history and child can do. She'd forced herself to interrupt their tête-à-tête, asking how long ago their reunion had been.

Mark looked at her apologetically. "We've been corresponding for a couple of years, since our accident and my diagnosis," he said, and Sylvia's knees buckled so she had to take the seat on the other side of his hospital bed.

"Why didn't you tell me? Was there something to hide?"

"No. No," Dierdre said. "It's just that we know how much you already have on your plate, and I've been trying to help Elaine with her singing career. We all know that I've failed as a parent." She looked at Mark. "And as a wife."

"Is it in her best interest to go into music?" Sylvia looked at Mark. "It's not a very stable career."

"That's why I called Deirdre. She's made it in the business." He turned toward Deirdre, excluding Sylvia from the circle again. "She can give our daughter guidance."

Ah. Elaine was *their* daughter. "And I'm just the substitute who has raised her for the past ten years." Sylvia glared at them, anxiety overtaking her and making her dizzy. Elaine had been an angry lost soul when Sylvia married Mark and taken the girl under her wing. Deirdre had abandoned her daughter to pursue her career on the road. Now Sylvia was the one who was to be abandoned. By Mark and by Elaine.

"It isn't like that," Mark said. "I love you. Elaine loves you. After I…" His voice cracked. "After I leave,

Elaine is going to need you more than ever. You and Deirdre."

Sylvia looked from one parent to the other. She saw Elaine's features in their faces—her mother's pert nose, her father's slow smile—and she relented. The child she had taken to her heart didn't need to know how betrayed she felt. Elaine didn't need to believe that Sylvia didn't support her dreams. She only prayed that Deirdre was true to her word—that she would watch over her daughter as she ventured into this fickle business.

"Okay, I'll support this," she said, turning toward Deirdre, "but you'd better swear to help where you can. She's very vulnerable right now."

"Thank you." Mark and Deidre breathed a sigh of relief, and Sylvia left the room to consider how to live with this new revelation.

A month later, she stood at Mark's graveside, tears streaming down her face, and recommitted to helping Elaine in the months that followed. She stood by, strong, and helped Elaine move forward with her life, facilitating the renewal of her stepdaughter's relationship with Deirdre. Sylvia supported Elaine as she launched her band, found an agent, and started playing on the national circuit. She helped Elaine until she could fly without Sylvia to hold her up. Only then had Sylvia fallen into deep grief and become consumed by depression.

"Well, hello again, Mrs. Tremblay." The surgeon interrupted her reverie. "How are you feeling?"

"Stupid, if you must know. I fell off a bike."

He chuckled at her rejoinder. "The surgery went well. We put in plates to hold the bone together, and it should heal fairly soon. You should stay off the leg for about four weeks, and I want you to come in for a follow-up appointment next week." She listened to him go on about the aftercare, about changing the bandages and watching for infection. "You can go home this morning. Do you have someone you would like us to call?"

"No. I have my phone." Who could she call? Elaine wasn't around. Alice lived three hours away and, after their earlier conversation, Sylvia didn't relish the idea of being carted all the way to Kamloops so her sister could harangue her for riding a bike. Maybe Isabella would be able to pick her up. She didn't know Isabella well, but she seemed like someone who might help.

Her cell phone rang then, and she reached for it, looking at the same unfamiliar number before answering the call.

"Sylvia." Jack's voice on the other end was a balm to her mounting anxiety. She calmly answered his anxious questions about her condition. "Do you have anyone to stay with you?" he finally asked.

"I don't think I'll need that. I've had a broken leg before, and I'm pretty self-sufficient." She didn't know if she was trying to convince him or herself.

"Why don't you stay with me for the first week?" He paused. "I mean, I have a guest room on the ground floor where my mother used to stay when she visited. It would just be for a week, until you begin to heal."

"But we hardly know each other."

"That's true. I guess I thought… or didn't think. At least let me drive you home."

"All right. I'd really appreciate it. They say I should be ready to go in about two hours."

"I'll be there," he said, and she sighed in relief. One problem solved.

WHEN JACK ARRIVED, the nurse

went over the aftercare instructions. "You'll need someone to drive you home and stay with you for at least twenty-four hours, preferably forty-eight, until you are able to get around for yourself."

"That's fine," Jack said. "I'll look after her."

"But Jack..."

"We'll discuss it later, Sylvia. Meanwhile, let's get you home." Jack pushed the wheelchair to the hospital entrance and helped Sylvia transfer from the chair to his car. He arranged her crutches in the back seat and climbed into the driver's seat.

"Listen," he said. "I know you want to go straight home, but I was thinking that I could have you stay in my guest room for a couple of days. I feel partially responsible, and the nurse did say that you should have someone around. My house is just a few blocks from here. Why not come for lunch and then decide?"

"I'm pretty tired," she said, and then looked at his crestfallen face. "But I'm also a little hungry. And you're right. It's probably best that I eat something."

Jack grinned and drove the few blocks to his home. "I've been watching the cooking channel the last couple of nights," he admitted. "I've made a great vegetable soup that you might enjoy."

"Lead on," she said, smiling. "I wouldn't miss it for the world."

~

JACK FORGOT Cassie was returning on Friday until she walked through the back door. "Hi, Dad. I've got great news," she said as she dropped her backpack on the floor and turned to the table he had set up for two. "Oh, you made us dinner."

"Well..." He tried to think of a way to explain that he hadn't remembered she was coming home. He didn't want to trigger a scene. Not with a witness...

A very special witness.

"What did you make?" Cassie crossed the floor to the stove and lifted the pot lids. "This looks great." She turned to look at him. "Where did you learn to cook?"

"I've had a tutor the past few days," he answered, nervous about how to tell her about Sylvia. He had to do it soon, so he might as well do it now… Or maybe in a few minutes. "What's your news?"

"I talked to Mom the other day. She's coming home."

Jack placed his hands on the counter and looked across at Cassie. "Your mother has been gone more than two years. She isn't coming back." Even if she did return, would he want her back?

"That's not true." Cassie thrust her chin out at him and glared at him. "She Skyped with me when I was away. She said she was coming here. To our house. To see us. She misses home."

"She hasn't been in touch with me," he said slowly. "She's probably coming to visit you, not me." He realized this was the truth. There was no way Emma was returning to their marriage.

"That's not what she told me," Cassie said, wandering around the kitchen. "Do you want me to dish up the food? It smells great. By the way, who is your tutor?"

He took a deep breath and said, "My friend Sylvia has been staying with me while she recovers from an accident, and..."

"There's another woman here?" Cassie turned toward him, her face stark with shock. "What about Mom?"

"I told you. Your mother hasn't been in contact with me since she left."

Cassie glared at him. "Who is this so-called friend of yours, anyway?"

"I am," a melodic voice said from the kitchen doorway. "Your father let me stay here for a few days until I get used to my crutches and can do for myself."

"And in return, Sylvia has been teaching me to cook," Jack added, waving his hand around the kitchen. "She's really good."

"Where did you two meet?" Cassie's face was red, and Jack braced himself for the angry outburst. He had seen the signs before.

"We met at the park," Sylvia said. "And your father has been gracious enough to let me stay for a few days after I had a mishap on my bicycle."

"She's been staying in the guest room downstairs," Jack added, "and today we're celebrating the fact that

Sylvia had a great check-up. No infection. Everything is mending as it should."

"And when will you be going home?" Cassie asked. Jack winced at the tone of her voice.

"Actually, your father was going to take me home this evening. I've been anxious to get back to my life —not that your help hasn't been welcome, Jack," she said.

Jack smiled at her. "It was a pleasure. I couldn't leave you alone to fend for yourself after you fell to avoid me." He wished they were alone and able to talk as they had the past few days. He saw in her eyes that she felt the same way.

Cassie cleared her throat and went to the cupboard and drawer to get another place setting. Jack knew that determined look in his daughter's eyes. They would have no further private time today.

"What do you do?" Cassie asked Sylvia as she sat down at the table.

"I took early retirement a few years ago, but before that I taught school," Sylvia answered. "Grade One, mostly."

"That's what I want to do," Cassie said and, by the time Jack joined them with a plate of grilled vegetable sandwiches, they were in a deep conversation about teaching. He watched as he ate and saw that Sylvia's generous nature was winning Cassie over just as it had with him.

Cassie came with them when Jack dropped Sylvia off at her home, and together they helped Sylvia into the house. Sylvia thanked Jack again for his hospitality.

"I'll be over tomorrow after work to see how you're getting on," Jack said, ignoring her protests.

She relented. "I'll be here. And maybe I'll have figured out how to get around enough to put together a dinner for you."

"I'd love to come for dinner." He kissed her on the cheek and noticed Cassie turning away. He hadn't meant to embarrass her. "I'm glad you're getting better," he said to Sylvia. "You still have to come on a train ride, remember?"

"I remember," she said, and leaned against the door jamb. The effort of getting up her front stairs had weakened her. He should go.

"I'll check in on you tomorrow."

At the bottom of the stairs, he turned to wave goodbye, and she was still there, watching him. *Damn*, but that felt good.

THE NEXT DAY, Sylvia lay in bed, staring at the ceiling and thinking about what she needed to do around the house. The bathrooms needed cleaning, the fridge needed stocking, and she had only a few hours until Jack arrived.

Smiling to herself, she got up and struggled to make the bed. Several minutes later she was successful and faced the task of washing and dressing. Her leg still ached, and as she struggled down the stairs, she decided to stay on the main floor for the next few weeks. She would sleep on the day bed in her office.

By five that evening, she had finished making dinner and was setting the table when Jack called.

"Sylvia, can I get a rain check on dinner tonight? Cassie called to say that she made dinner for me—my favourite—and asked what time I was coming home."

"I see." Sylvia's buoyant mood plummeted.

"I'll be over after dinner, though," he said. "Cassie's been away for a few days and seems to be feeling left out. "

What had she expected? He had a daughter, just like Mark had. Cassie, like Elaine, was her father's whole world. "Well, why not come over for dessert, then?" she asked hopefully. *Have you no shame?* The ANTs were back again. She hadn't even noticed their absence until now.

"Do you mind if I bring Cassie?" he asked tentatively. "I mean, if she decides that she wants to come?"

"Of course not. I made a lovely apple pie and ice cream. I can't eat the whole thing myself."

"We… I'll be there," Jack said. "I love apple pie."

"I'll see you around six thirty."

JACK BEGAN to walk toward home. Cassie had called only an hour earlier, out of the blue and out of breath, insisting that he come straight home.

"I have a surprise for you," she said.

"What kind of a surprise?" he had asked warily. Cassie's surprises were not always good, and lately her refrain was that she wanted to go back to school in Kelowna. He hoped she wouldn't go to much trouble to change his mind. The week without her hadn't been as bad as he had feared, and he knew he would manage when she returned to school. For the first time in two years, he was looking forward to his future—and he hoped it included Sylvia.

He walked into the kitchen, noticed three place settings on the table, and smiled. Sylvia had sounded surprised and sad that he wouldn't be there for dinner, and meanwhile, she was planning to be here the whole time. He would have to remember not to play poker with her. She was an excellent actor.

Deciding two could play at this game, he delayed going into the living room to greet her, choosing instead to go upstairs to shower and change. He didn't want to ruin their surprise.

A few minutes later, he bounded down the stairway to the living room, pausing two stairs from the bottom to stare at the woman sitting there.

"Hello, Jack," Emma said. She was in the chair facing the stairs. Her chair. Jack felt like a ton of bricks had slammed into his chest and nearly lost his footing on the last two steps.

He looked at her and wondered for a moment if the last three years had been a dream. Her face, the same one he had looked at every morning for thirty years, was there smiling at him, knowing him, as lovely as ever.

"Emma. What are you doing here? I thought you were in Spain."

"She's come home to visit, Dad." Cassie made air quotes with her fingers around the word *visit* and smiled happily at them.

"I see. So this was your surprise?" he asked Cassie, still looking at Emma.

"I came to talk to you, Jack." Emma said. "Cassie invited me to dinner, and we've spent the afternoon catching up."

"I see," Jack said, remembering that Sylvia had used these same words with him not two hours earlier.

"Shall we have dinner?" Cassie asked, clearly pleased that the two of them were in the same room. "It's been forever since we had a family dinner together."

Emma looked at Jack, and Jack looked at Emma.

"Yes, let's eat," Emma finally said, speaking for them both. She hadn't changed. She still felt entitled to speak on his behalf and make decisions that included him without his consent. He followed them to the table Cassie had set with the best china, and they sat in their familiar chairs. He felt awkward as they passed platters around the table.

"You've been looking after yourself, Jack," Emma said, looking him up and down. "You've lost some weight, and Cassie says you've been walking more."

"Dad's been learning to cook too." Cassie handed Jack the potatoes. "He made the most delicious sandwich for me yesterday."

Emma's eyebrows rose as she looked at him. "Well, that's a switch. You've been making some changes."

Jack cut into his chicken and took a bite, chewing slowly, while he thought of what else to say. Had they always carried on conversations as though he were nothing but a puppet they provided words for? He listened to their conversation as he choked down bite after bite of food. Finally, the meal was over. Hopefully that meant Emma would leave soon.

"I thought you would have sold this place by now," Emma said as Cassie bustled in the kitchen, getting the coffee. "Isn't it too much for one person to look after?"

"Well, there are two of us living here right now," Jack answered. "I thought Cassie had enough of changes. When she lost her mother, she didn't need to lose the house she grew up in as well." Emma's lips pressed together tightly, and he knew his words had hit home.

"But she's going back to school in the fall. What will you do then?"

"I'll manage." He glared at her. "Where's Lorenzo?"

"Lorenzo's downtown. He had a conference in town, and I came with him."

"I see." He paused as Cassie backed through the door between the kitchen and the dining room and turned to place a tray with two coffee cups, cream and sugar, spoons, and some homemade cookies onto the table.

"Aren't you joining us?" he asked as she began to walk toward the front door.

"Oh, I thought I would go for a run while you two talk," Cassie said. "I'll be back by seven."

Jack and Emma watched as the door closed behind their daughter.

"Tell me, Emma. Exactly why are you here?"

IT WAS six thirty when Sylvia's doorbell rang.

"Right on time." She did love that about Jack. He was dependable.

She swung herself on to her crutches and hurried to the front door to find Cassie standing there, iPod on, earbuds in.

"Hi, Sylvia," she said as she removed her earbuds. "I was out for a run and thought I would stop by to see how you were doing."

"Thanks," Sylvia said, looking past Cassie to the street. "Is your father with you?"

"Oh, he's home with Mom," Cassie said blithely. "She came home today. She's missed us and has decided to come back."

"I see." *I told you so. No one wants you.*

She screamed at her depressing thoughts to stop.

"I thought I would come to see how you're getting on now that you're back home."

Sylvia smiled at Cassie, seeing so much of Elaine in this girl. The last thing Sylvia wanted to be was a home wrecker.

"I've made a few adjustments, but I'm managing. I even got outside for some fresh air this afternoon. Such nice weather."

"And you've been cooking," Cassie said, sniffing the air.

"Yes, I've even made an apple pie. I thought that it would be a good way to use up some of the old apples I had in the fridge. Most everything else had to be thrown out. But I was able to get food delivered from the local market. It was something I did often when Mark, my husband, was sick, and I couldn't get out to shop."

"I didn't know you were married."

"He died over two years ago. Cancer."

"Oh, I'm sorry." The smile Cassie wore slipped a bit before she added, "I'm glad you're doing well, Sylvia. I should be going. I told them I would be home by seven, and I still have a few kilometers to run before I'm finished."

"Thank you for stopping by, and please tell your father I'm fine. No need to worry about me," Sylvia said, closing and bolting the door and swinging her way back to the kitchen.

She sliced into the pie, cutting herself a big piece, and poured herself a large cup of decaf coffee before perching on a stool near the counter, putting her head into her hands, and sobbing. She was alone again, looking from the outside at a family reunited at her expense.

No use crying over spilled milk. Her mother's voice cut through the tears. She was startled into silence. The voice was back. She had to stamp out the negative thoughts.

"I'm getting better. This is just a little setback. He was lonely, and so was I. I'm sure it wouldn't have worked out anyway."

She raised her head and looked at the big piece of pie in front of her. She'd been eating so well the past few weeks.

Sylvia placed the slice back into the slot where it came from and then cut the pie into several more slices before covering it with plastic wrap and putting it into a basket. She was going to take the pie next door to her neighbor, who had three teenaged boys: a thank-you for all the times they had shoveled snow off her driveway.

She left her cell phone on the counter while she was away, and missed three calls: the first from Alice, the second from Jack, and the last from Elaine. She returned only two of those calls when she came home.

~

JACK WAITED for Emma to answer him and felt long-forgotten anger rise in his chest. She had left him. She had stood right there and told him she was leaving, letting him figure out how to pick up the pieces when she walked out the door.

"I'm here to talk about Cassie. You can't keep her tied to you. She needs to go and get herself a life."

"What makes you think I'm tying her down, or that I even could?"

"She makes dinner for you every night. I know she said that you were learning to cook, but Jack, we both know that's not true. She's fooling herself, covering for you."

"Emma, if that's why you've come all this way, then you've wasted your time."

"Did you spend all of her college

fund? Is that why you won't let her go back to school?"

"You still don't listen, do you? I am not keeping Cassie from going back to school. She's already registered to go back in September."

"But she's reluctant to leave you. Worried you won't be able to handle things on your own."

"I can handle things just fine," he roared. "Not that it's any of your business what I do."

"It's my business when it concerns our daughter and her future." Emma raised her voice and stood at the other end of the dining room table. "I don't want her life to be like mine was."

Jack felt as though she had sucker-punched him for the second time that day. "Was living with me so awful? I thought we were happy."

"I swore I would never end up like my mother. I'd never be home nursing someone instead of grabbing life by the tail. I built my career so I'd never have to do that. And then when you got sick, well…"

"When I got sick you realized that you had made a mistake marrying me, is that it?"

"No." She walked over to the window and peered outside. "No, I can't regret marrying you, or I wouldn't have Cassie. She's a wonderful girl. We raised her well, you and I."

"Great. So the only reason you're happy I came along is so I could give you a child?" The pain of her earlier rejection tore into him again.

"Not exactly." She stood and pondered a moment. "You were a better man than my father."

"Joseph Stalin was a better man than your father. He was a drunk, a sloth, downright nasty, and well… it doesn't really bear going into, does it?"

"You were stable. You were good to me and to our daughter. You never had an unkind word to say to either of us. You were too good for me."

"You left because I was too good? What was wrong with me? What did you need me to do, to be? I don't understand."

She stood for a few more minutes before saying softly, "It wasn't you who was wrong, and it wasn't me, either." She waved her hand back and forth between them. "It was us. We didn't work anymore. Together we were less than we were apart. You weren't inspiring me to be better, and I wasn't inspiring you. We were old hat. Stale. And no matter what I tried to do to breathe life back into our marriage, it didn't seem to work. I'm sorry I hurt you. I'm sorry that I left the way I did."

"Things aren't all roses and rainbows with Lorenzo?"

"No." She laughed. "Lorenzo is too mercurial for that. Too passionate. But he pushes me. He makes me try harder. I'm always a little off-balance with him, and I like that."

"I don't really want to hear about Lorenzo's passion."

"I keep him off-balance too," she

said. “I think he likes a woman who stands up to him.”

“I wish you well with him.” And he was surprised to find that he really did.

“He’ll be here to get me in a few minutes. I hope Cassie returns before that. I’d like her to meet him. She said she would be back by seven.”

“Seven.” He looked at his watch. Six fifty-five.

Sylvia. He’d told her he’d be there at six thirty. “Excuse me a moment, I have a quick call to make.” He dialled the number, and it went to voicemail. Where would she be? Perhaps the bathroom, or maybe she left her phone in her pocket in another room. He walked into the kitchen long enough to leave a voicemail message.

"Sylvia, I'm sorry I wasn't able to make it for dessert this evening. A family… emergency came up. I'll call you later to see how you are."

He returned to the living room to find Cassie and her mother in conversation.

"What do you mean? Lorenzo is coming here? Why would I want to meet him?"

"I thought you might like to meet your new stepfather."

"Stepfather? But you left him. You've come home for good."

"Why would you think that? Lorenzo and I are very happy together."

"No. That can't be true. You said you wanted to talk to Dad." Cassie paced the floor, and Jack stood back, watching the interaction, unsure how, or if, to intercede. Too late, Cassie saw him hovering.

"Dad, tell her you want her back. Tell her to come home."

"I can't make her do what she doesn't want to do. And your mother is right. Our marriage is over—has been for a long time." Was that a look of gratitude he saw in Emma's eyes?

"You should try harder! Tell her how much you've learned in the last few months about cooking, about doing things around the house. Tell her how much you've changed."

He walked over to Cassie, who was now in tears, and took her into his arms. "Cassie, as much as you want your mother and me to be together, it just can't be any longer. She's with Lorenzo now. She has a new life in Spain. My life is here."

Cassie tore herself away from him and hissed, "Is this because of that woman, that Sylvia?"

"Who's Sylvia?" Emma asked.

"Sylvia is a friend of mine," Jack said quietly. "She's a woman I've been spending time with over the past few weeks."

"She's been living here for the past week!" Cassie said, her voice rising.

"No," Jack said firmly. "She stayed here with me for a few days while she healed from her surgery. She broke her leg, and her doctors advised that she not be alone for the first while. I felt responsible for her accident because she fell off her bike to avoid running into me. She stayed in the guest bedroom." He found himself on the defensive, even though he didn't need to explain this to anyone, least of all Emma. "She stayed until she was able to wield her crutches on her own, and meanwhile she taught me a few things about cooking."

"What is she like, this Sylvia?" Emma asked.

"She's a nice woman, a widow. She loves walking in the gardens at the park, loves wildlife, and she can cook. Boy, can she cook." He smiled as he remembered the last time he had seen her. She was a great kisser too, but damned if he would share that with these two.

"So you like her?" Emma said, watching him closely.

"What's not to like?"

"Sylvia doesn't need you any-more, Dad. She told me to tell you that she's just fine," Cassie interrupted.

"When did you talk to Sylvia?" Jack's heart pounded.

"I went over there after dinner. Told her Mom was back. She seemed happy to hear you were back together."

"Why would you say that?" her mother asked her. "Cassie, Lorenzo has asked me to marry him."

"You aren't back, then? You aren't coming home again?"

"No," Emma and Jack said together. It was probably the first time they had agreed on anything in a very long time.

"No, not in the way you would

like me to be," Emma continued. "Though Lorenzo has agreed to spend more time in Canada. I miss you." Emma smiled at them both. "Lorenzo will be here any minute. I'd like you both to meet him. It would mean a lot to me."

Cassie sank into the nearby couch. She looked small and fragile, more so than Jack had ever seen her. A horn sounded from the driveway.

"Please come and meet him, Cassie," her mother urged.
"For me?"

Cassie sighed deeply, rose, and went outside to meet Lorenzo. He, in turn, was charming, something Jack had never really been. Lorenzo even managed to squeeze a promise from Cassie to visit Spain during school break that November. Emma beamed at them.

Before they left, Emma crossed the driveway to speak to Jack.

"I'm pleased to hear you're dating again. And you look well. I'm sorry I accused you of holding Cassie back. Please accept my apology."

"Thank you," Jack said, then kissed her on both cheeks and said goodbye.

Jack stood with Cassie while she waved them off.

"Dad, why didn't you fight for her?" she asked.

"Your mother isn't a prize to be won, Cassie. She's an individual with a mind of her own. She chose him. We need to accept that."

"Oh, Dad," she wailed and ran

into the house and up to her room, slamming the door behind her.

Well, there was no going out tonight. The last thing Cassie needed today was to think that her father was abandoning her too. He needed to talk to someone. And the only person he really wanted to see was Sylvia.

He dialed her number, but the phone went straight to voicemail. He left another message and put the phone down. He'd need to make it up to Sylvia, and despite what he had just told his daughter about not fighting for a woman, he realized he would fight dragons for Sylvia. What was that woman doing to him? She'd only been in his life a few weeks, but she'd already made a home in his heart.

SEVEN

SYLVIA WAS GOING to visit her sister Alice. It had been a long time since she had been to Kamloops, the town where they had grown up. She limped around the bedroom, packing her clothes, and carefully rolled the suitcase while leaning on one crutch.

"I can do this," she said to herself. She was soon in the cab on the way to the airport.

When she landed in Kamloops, Alice swept Sylvia into a hug and held her. "It is good to see you, Syl. You look fantastic!"

"I do, don't I?" Sylvia answered. She had lost fifteen pounds in the past month and, despite her leg, felt healthier than she had in years.

"How long can you stay?"

"I'm here for two weeks, but then I need to get back. Isabella is going to Oregon to run a half marathon in early August. I need to be home to feed Angel."

"Angel. A very good name for that cat. She's certainly been an angel for you."

The visit with Alice was just what Sylvia needed. She spent time with her nieces and nephew while Alice was at work, cooked dinner

for the family every night, and felt
generally useful. She thought often of Jack, but pushed him out of her mind during her active days and found herself dropping quickly off to sleep every night, tired from all the activity. She was almost sorry to leave.

"I wish you could live here always," her fourteen-year-old nephew, James, said to her when they were seeing her off at the airport.

"I'll come back soon to visit. I promise. But right now, I need to get home."

"To feed Angel," her little niece, Elizabeth, piped up. "Aunty has to feed the kitty."

"Yes, exactly," Sylvia answered, kissing the children and giving

ge hug. "Thanks for let-
ay. It was good to see

You can come anytime. I haven't cooked at all. You really should go on that Italian tour you've always talked about."

"Maybe I will," she said.

She visited her doctor when she returned and was deemed ready for a walking cast. Glad to be able to trade her crutches for a cane, Sylvia walked a few blocks every day, feeling the strength return to her leg. She was pleased to take over Angel's feeding when Isabella left on her trip.

The afternoon before Isabella's flight, they met for a few minutes in the park.

Isabella smiled her usual broad

smile. "Thank you for letting me help Angel. I feel like a new woman."

"You look like a new woman too," Sylvia said. "I barely recognized you!"

Isabella chuckled. "That's what George said when I saw him last week. He's an old friend of my husband's. We've been dating." She blushed.

"Good for you." Sylvia was pleased for her friend. "Have fun at the race."

"I will," Isabella said as she hugged Sylvia to her. "Wish me luck beating my time."

"Luck!" Sylvia said. "Wishing you lots of luck."

Isabella jogged down the path, and Sylvia sat on the bench to fill the cat dish and set it on the bench beside her. Angel was much braver now, jumping up onto the bench to eat her fill.

"Well, well," a deep voice said from behind her left ear. "I never would have believed it if I hadn't seen it with my own eyes."

Jack was standing beside her. She smiled tentatively up at him.

"My mother used to say that a lot can be accomplished if you are patient."

He walked around the bench to face her. "How have you been? I tried to call you several times, but I seem to have missed you. I wanted to explain about—"

"No need to explain," Sylvia said. "Cassie told me that your wife came home. I wish you well."

"That's just it," Jack said. "Cassie misunderstood the situation. Wishful thinking, I suppose. Emma isn't back. She only came to lecture me about my treatment of our daughter and to introduce her fiancé to Cassie."

"Her fiancé?"

"She and Lorenzo are to be married. It's taken a couple of weeks, but I think Cassie is finally accepting that our marriage is over. Cassie's going to travel to Spain to see where her mother lives."

"Your wife hasn't returned, then?"

"Ex-wife. No, our marriage is over. Dead."

"I see," Sylvia said.

"Do you?" Jack asked. "Sylvia,

I'm so sorry if you were hurt by this. I just wanted you to know that."

"You must be on your way to the train," Sylvia said.

"Yes, I am. I have another couple of runs to do before we close for the day. Can I call you later?" He looked so hopeful and her heart beat faster.

"No, I mean... Well, I was hoping... You still owe me a train ride," she said.

He reached over to squeeze her hand. "Yes, I do. Come on."

JACK LED the way to the train and listened as Sylvia told him of her visit with her sister. He could listen to her all day and not tire of it. After driving the train twice around the track, he brought it to a smooth halt outside the station to off-load the children. Tyler was waiting for him.

"Hi, Tyler. You about ready for dinner?" He turned to Sylvia. "Tyler and I are going to try out that new restaurant at the edge of the park tonight."

"No can do. I have a dentist appointment," Tyler answered.

Jack narrowed his eyes at his young friend. "I didn't know you had an appointment."

"Just made it." Tyler held up his cell phone. "They had a cancellation, and they were able to fit me in. Rain check?"

Jack swallowed an exasperated sigh and turned to Sylvia. "Would you care to join me for dinner?"

Sylvia blinked at Jack. She'd been

watching the exchange. "I-I…" She paused and looked into his eyes.

"Say yes," he said. "This ungrateful cur is abandoning me to my own devices, and I hate to eat alone."

"All right, then. Yes."

He resisted the urge to hug her. "I'll see you tomorrow, Tyler."

But Tyler was already on his way to the parking lot, and Jack could swear he heard him whistling.

They entered the restaurant, and Sylvia clapped her hands together in excitement. "It's Italian," she said. "I'm going to Italy in two months. I booked my ticket yesterday."

"So, you'll be taking your culinary tour after all."

"Oh, yes. And then, perhaps, I'll

look for a job cooking in a restaurant like this one."

They spent the next several minutes looking through the menu, and the next hour flew by as they caught up.

"I've missed you." He took her hand in both of his.

"I've missed you too."

"Do you think we could start over—try this all again?"

"I'd rather just pick up where we left off," she said. "First dates are so awkward."

"I'd like that."

THREE MONTHS LATER, Jack stood at the airport arrivals gate and grinned when he saw Sylvia walking toward him.

"How was your trip?" he asked.

"My trip was wonderful." She let him fold her into his arms. "But it's so much better to be home."

THANK YOU!

Dear Reader,

Thank you for reading ***Love's Fresh Start,*** the first Sunshine Bay story.

I hope you enjoyed it!

To be the first to get news about future stories from Sunshine Bay head over to my website (http://JeanineLauren.com) to sign up for my newsletter.

If you enjoyed the story, please consider taking a few moments to leave a review. Reviews are a fabulous way to support authors so we can continue to write more books for you to enjoy.

The next installment of the Sunshine Bay series is scheduled to come out later this year.

Until next time,

Jeanine Lauren

ABOUT THE AUTHOR

Jeanine Lauren has always loved a good story. She prefers those where the strength of community and the power of love combine to overcome even the darkest of situations.

Jeanine writes from her home in the lower mainland of British Columbia, Canada, not far from the fictional town of Sunshine Bay, where many of her characters live.

Made in the USA
San Bernardino, CA
13 May 2020